THE MAGIC TOY SHOP

Contributing Writer
Carolyn Quattrocki

Illustrations
Susan Spellman

Publications International, Ltd.

Cornelius was a toymaker. He was very busy in his toy shop. "Only two more days left before Christmas," he said to himself, "and I still have all these toys to finish. I'm not as young as I used to be, and I can't work as fast. I just hope I'll be able to finish them in time."

The boys and girls in the town couldn't wait to receive their Christmas toys. And Cornelius had made a special one for each child he knew.

Just then, Cornelius's wife, Katerina, came into the shop to call him home for his dinner. "I can't stop now. I must keep working," said Cornelius, "at least until I finish this toy train. Little Charles will be very disappointed if he doesn't have his train for Christmas."

Cornelius pointed to a princess doll and a pair of skates he had just finished. "At least those are ready for Caroline and little Tommy," he said.

At that moment, the shop door opened. A poor woman came into the shop with her three children. The children's eyes opened wide as they gazed at the toys and games.

Peter wished he could have the toy train for his very own. Lisa wanted the beautiful doll. Little Karen touched the cuddly, pink bunny. But the mother had only a few pennies to spend, certainly not enough for these wonderful toys.

After the children and their mother left, Katerina said, "Why don't we give the children the toys they want, as a special Christmas gift, even if they can't pay for them?"

But Cornelius shook his head sadly. "I wish we could, but those toys are already promised. And I have no time to make any others." So the toymaker and his wife closed the shop and went home to their dinner.

After Cornelius and Katerina left, the toys in the little shop suddenly seemed to awaken and come to life. They began talking among themselves. They all had heard and seen the poor children wishing for Christmas toys.

Then Harold, one of the most handsome of the toy soldiers, had an idea. "We can help. More than anyone, we know all about toys. *We* can make special Christmas gifts for the children!"

But Louisa, the beautiful doll, said, "What a foolish idea! I have never done any work before, and I won't begin now. You silly toys go right ahead, but don't count on me!"

She walked over to the corner of the toy shelf and watched as the other toys began to work. Two toy soldiers were already busy putting together the engine of a toy train. And Brown Bear was sewing up the sides of a pink, furry bunny.

Then Louisa looked up to see two taffy-colored kittens trying to paint a face on a princess doll. "Goodness," thought Louisa. "They're making a terrible mess of it! Maybe I *had* better help them, just a *little*."

Louisa shooed the kittens away and set to work herself. In a while, one of the kittens said, "Oooh, how beautiful you've made her—just as beautiful as you are!" Louisa smiled and patted the kittens on the head.

When Cornelius and Katerina opened their shop the next day, they saw three toys they had never seen before: a train with a tag that said *For Peter;* a princess doll with a tag that said *For Lisa;* and a pink stuffed bunny whose tag said *For Karen.* Where had they come from? Something *magical* must have happened!

That evening, Cornelius gave the three children their wonderful Christmas gifts.

Cornelius and Katerina did not come to their shop the next day, because it was Christmas. They stayed home to eat their own special Christmas dinner.

But the day after Christmas, Cornelius took down the sign over the door of the toy shop. "I must change the name of my shop," he said. "I will make a new sign. From now on, my shop will not be called The Toy Shop. It will be The *Magic* Toy Shop!"